A SONG FOR JESS

John Cunliffe

Illustrated by Jane Hickson from the
Television Designs by Ivor Wood

ANDRE DEUTSCH CHILDREN'S BOOKS

Scholastic Children's Books
Scholastic Publications Ltd
7-9 Pratt Street, London NW1 0AE, UK

Scholastic Inc
730 Broadway, New York, NY 10003, USA

Scholastic Canada Ltd
123 Newkirk Road, Richmond Hill
Ontario, Canada L4C 3G5

Ashton Scholastic Pty Ltd
PO Box 579, Gosford, New South Wales
Australia

Ashton Scholastic Ltd
Private Bag 1, Penrose, Auckland
New Zealand

First published in the UK by Scholastic Publication
Ltd, 1992

ISBN: 0 590 54046 7

Typeset by Rapid Reprographics, London
Printed by Proost International Ltd

When Pat was in the bath he loved to sing.
Oh, how he sang!

Jess did *not* like Pat's song.
Not a bit. He hated it!
It made his fur stand on end.
It made his tail go up like a flag-post.

Jess ran away from Pat's song. He ran into the garden.

A blackbird was singing in a tree. It sang a lovely song. Jess liked this song, but it made him feel very hungry.

He climbed the tree to catch the blackbird.
The blackbird flew away, and Jess got all scratched and rumpled climbing down the tree again.

Pat was still singing.

Jess ran across the fields until he came to a stream. The water sang a song that Jess liked. It gurgled, and splashed, and rippled over the stones. Jess saw a fish in a deep pool. It looked quiet where the fish was. Jess thought the fish would be nice to eat.

He dipped his paw in the water to catch the fish. He slipped and fell - *splash* - into the pool. Oh, how Jess hated getting wet.

He jumped out of the water, and
shook himself until he was dry.
He didn't like the water's song now.

It was getting dark, and time for Jess to go home.

Pat had finished his bath and his song. The moon was coming out. Pat looked out of the window, and said, "Oooooh, what a noise!"
There was a howling, wailing, crying sound in the dark garden. It made Pat's hair stand on end. "It's Jess," said Sara, "singing to his girl-friends."

Pat called to Jess and rattled
his dish...
"Come on, Jess, time for supper!"

19

Jess was still hungry. So he ended *his* song, too, and came indoors. Something was cooking on the stove, and the pans sang their own quiet song.

"That's better," said Pat.

23

"That's better," thought Jess, as he lapped up his milk.